ISBN: 1-40372-352-4
15241/0406 Puppies for Sale

Printed in the U.S.A.

06 07 08 09 BNG 10 9 8 7 6 5 4 3 2 1

PUPPIES FOR SALE

WRITTEN BY DAN CLARK

ILLUSTRATED BY JERRY DILLINGHAM

A store owner

was tacking a

sign in his store

window which read

PUPPIES FOR SALE,

when a little

boy appeared.

"How much are you

selling the puppies

for?" he asked.

The man told the

lad he didn't expect to

let any of them go for

less than fifty dollars.

The boy
reached in his
pocket, pulled
out some change,
looked up at the
store owner and
said, "I have two
dollars and thirty-
seven cents. Can
I look at them?"

The store owner

smiled and whistled.

From the kennel,

a dog named Lady

came running down

the aisle, followed

by five tiny

balls of fur.

One puppy

lagged behind.

Immediately,

the little boy

asked about the

limping puppy.

"What's wrong

with the doggie?"

"The veterinarian told us the dog is missing a hip socket," said the store owner. "He'll always limp like that."

"That's the one

I want to buy,"

the lad said quickly.

The store owner

replied, "No, you

don't want to

buy that dog. If

you really want

him, I'll just give

him to you."

The boy came close to the store owner's face and said angrily, "I don't want you to just give him to me.

That doggie is worth just as much as all the other puppies and I'll pay the full price. In fact, I'll give you two dollars and thirty-seven cents now and fifty cents a month until I have him paid for!"

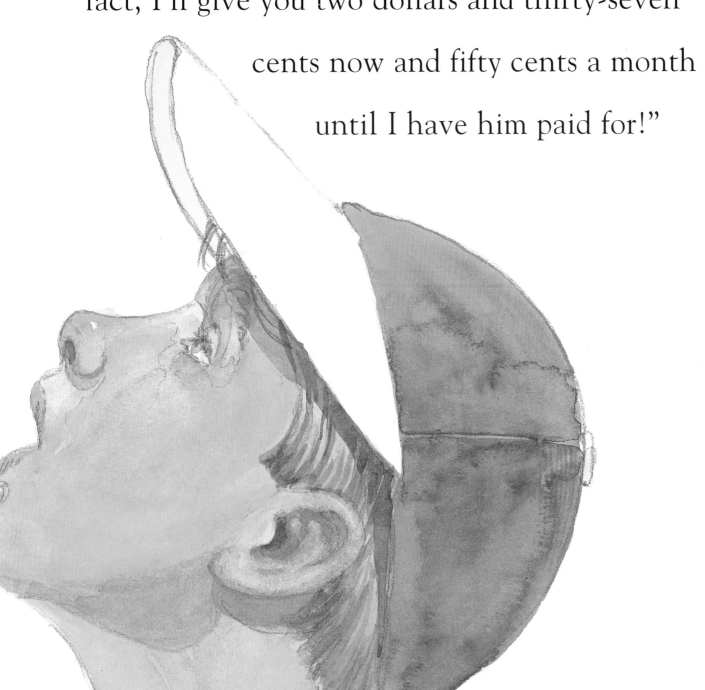

The store owner

replied, "No, no, no.

You don't want that

dog. He's never going

to be able to run and

jump and play like

the other dogs."

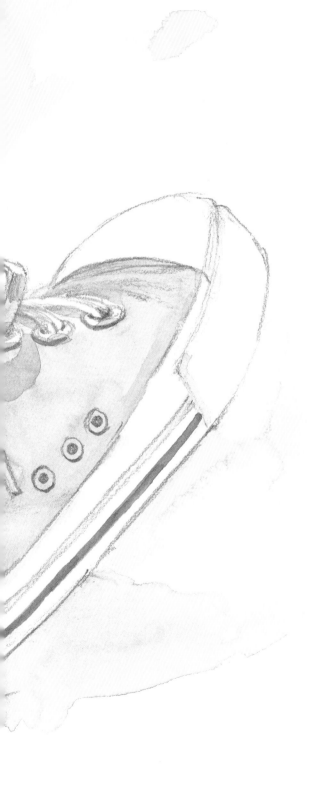

In response, the

little boy pulled

up his pant leg

to reveal a badly

twisted right leg,

supported by two

steel braces.

"Well, sir," he said,

"I don't run so well

myself and the puppy

will need someone

who understands."